CHRIS BLAKE

TIME HUNTERS

GREEK WARRIORS

HarperCollins *Children's Books*

KU-074-786

Travel through time with Tom and Isis
on more

adventures!

LIVEWIRE WARRINGTON	
34143101320248	
Bertrams	09/07/2013
JF	£5.99
CUL	

For games, competitions and more visit:

www.time-hunters.com

CONTENTS

PROLOGUE

Five thousand years ago

Princess Isis and her pet cat, Cleo, stood outside the towering carved gates to the Afterlife. It had been rotten luck to fall off a pyramid and die at only ten years of age, but Isis wasn't worried – the Afterlife was meant to be great. People were dying to go there, after all! Her mummy's wrappings were so uncomfortable she couldn't wait a second longer to get in, get her body back and wear normal clothes again.

"Oi, Aaanuuubis, Anubidooby!" Isis shouted impatiently. "When you're ready, you old dog!"

Cleo started to claw Isis's shoulder. Then she yowled, jumping from Isis's arms and cowering behind her legs.

"Calm down, fluffpot," Isis said, bending to stroke her pet. "He can't exactly woof me to death!" The princess laughed, but froze when she stood up. Now she understood what Cleo had been trying to tell her.

Looming up in front of her was the enormous jackal-headed god of the Underworld himself, Anubis. He was so tall that Isis's neck hurt to look up at him. He glared down his long snout at her with angry red eyes. There was nothing pet-like about him. Isis gulped.

"'WHEN YOU'RE READY, YOU OLD DOG?'" Anubis growled. "'ANUBIDOOBY?'"

Isis gave the god of the Underworld a winning smile and held out five shining amulets. She had been buried with them so she could give them to Anubis to gain entry to the Afterlife. There was a sixth amulet too – a gorgeous green one. But Isis had hidden it under her arm. Green *was* her favourite colour, and surely Anubis didn't need all six.

Except the god didn't seem to agree. His fur bristled in rage. "FIVE? Where is the sixth?" he demanded.

Isis shook her head. "I was only given five," she said innocently.

To her horror, Anubis grabbed the green amulet from its hiding place. "You little LIAR!" he bellowed.

Thunder started to rumble. The ground shook. Anubis snatched all six amulets and tossed them into the air. With a loud crack and a flash of lightning, they vanished.

"You hid them from me!" he boomed. "Now I have hidden them from you – in the most dangerous places throughout time."

Isis's bandaged shoulders drooped in despair. "So I c-c-can't come into the Afterlife then?"

"Not until you have found each and every

one. But first, you will have to get out of this..." Anubis clicked his fingers. A life-sized pottery statue of the goddess Isis, whom Isis was named after, appeared before him.

Isis felt herself being sucked into the statue, along with Cleo. "What are you doing to me?" she yelled.

"You can only escape if somebody breaks the statue," Anubis said. "So you'll have plenty of time to think about whether trying to trick the trickster god himself was a good idea!"

The walls of the statue closed around Isis, trapping her and Cleo inside. The sound of Anubis's evil laughter would be the last sound they would hear for a long, long time...

CHAPTER 1
SUPERMARKET SWEEP

The old lady's shopping trolley was closing in on Isis Amun-Ra and her cat, Cleopatra.

Tom watched in horror.

"Get out of the way!" he shouted to Isis, waving his arms.

But the mummified Ancient Egyptian princess just stood at the entrance of the supermarket, hands on her hips, and said, "Why?"

The old lady wheeled her trolley straight

at the two Egyptians.

Tom ran over and pushed his friends out of the trolley's path.

"Are you trying to get killed?" he squeaked.

"Don't be silly!" Isis said cheerfully. "I'm already dead."

She ran in and out of the supermarket's automatic doors, making them open and close.

"Stop! People are staring," Tom hissed.

"Not at me!" Isis laughed. "Nobody but you can see us. Cleo and I are pretty nifty on our feet for five thousand years old, aren't we?"

Suddenly Isis squealed. She pointed at Tom's mother, who was pushing a supermarket trolley with a wonky wheel towards them.

"Look, Fluffpot!" she cried. Our very own chariot!"

"Tom," Mum said. "I thought I told you to wait by the trolleys!"

"That's right, you naughty boy," said Isis, wagging her finger at Tom. "You should listen to mummy."

Tom groaned and shot Isis a look of frustration. Under his breath he muttered, "I've been listening to a mummy ever since I broke that statue."

A few weeks earlier, Tom had accidentally broken a statue of the goddess Isis at the museum where his dad worked, releasing the mummies of Isis and Cleo, who had been trapped inside it for over five thousand years. And now Tom was stuck with them until they'd found all six amulets that Anubis had scattered throughout history.

"Shopping's so boring!" Tom grumbled, as they passed under the neon-lit entrance to the supermarket. "Why did I have to come?" he whined to Mum.

Mum was busy checking her list. "I need you to push the trolley," she said, wandering over to the fruit and vegetable section.

Tom grabbed the trolley's handle. But just as he was about to stop next to the tomatoes and peppers, Isis shouted. "Come on, Cleo! Let's ride the chariot!"

Cleo mewed heartily. The two climbed up on to the banana shelf and sprang into the trolley, with Cleo nestling in the front section and Isis perched on the child's seat.

Isis reached up and pulled down some bunting that was advertising the bananas. She flung it round Tom's body and gave it a yank.

"Giddy-up, horsey! Pull me and Cleo to victory! YAH!"

"Isis, no!" Tom said.

"What's wrong?" Isis asked. "You said you were bored. I'm only trying to liven things up a bit. I thought we could play chariot races."

Just as Tom was about to tell Isis what he thought of her pretending he was a horse, the supermarket manager loomed over him. He knew it was the manager because the red-faced man wore a badge that said: 'Brian, Store Manager' on it.

Brian tapped Tom on the shoulder. "Young man! You are not to play with the bunting!" He pulled the tangle of yellow triangles off Tom's coat.

Then, worst of all, Mum came over.

"Tom! What on earth are you doing?"

Her face was pink with embarrassment. She waved a bunch of celery in the air, almost hitting Brian on the head. She turned to him and bit her lip. "I'm so sorry. He's normally such a sensible boy."

Tom glared at Isis. He was sure she was smirking under her bandages.

"Blah blah blah blah *sensible boy*!" Isis's impression of Mum was spot on. She giggled as Tom stormed off, pushing the trolley towards the meat counter.

"You'd better behave yourself now!" Tom hissed at Isis when Mum wasn't looking.

"Wheeeee!" she shouted, as Tom rounded a corner. "I wiiiiill!"

They pushed on towards the frozen food section. To Tom's horror, as they turned into the coldest aisle in the shop, Isis grabbed an enormous pack of toilet roll from a shelf. She tore the pack open and started to wrap white toilet paper round herself.

"What on earth are you doing now?" Tom cried. "You're already all bandaged up."

Isis tutted loudly. "K-keeping warm. It's f-freezing in here. Do you want me to f-freeze to death?"

"You're already dead, as you just
reminded me!" Tom said.

Isis ignored him and carried on unwinding
the toilet roll.

Tom was frustrated by her pranks.

"I know you *think* you're hilarious, but every bit of mischief *you* get into, gets *me* into trouble!" he said.

"What? Like this?" Isis tossed a toilet roll at Tom's head. She giggled as it bounced off him.

"Yes. That's exactly what I mean!" Tom said.

"Fetch me a packet of fish fingers, will you, Tom?" said Mum. "And do stop talking to yourself. You sound like Dad."

Tom leaned over the freezer, and gasped as the ground began to shake. Shoppers carried on pushing their trolleys down the aisle as if nothing was happening, but Tom knew it could mean only one thing...

"Anubis!" Isis yelped. She clutched Cleo close to her.

"I guess we're off on our next adventure!"

20

Tom said, gulping. "Look!" He pointed at
the jackal's head that was emerging from
beneath the frozen vegetables.

Isis peeped into the freezer. "I d–d–don't care
where he sends us," she said through chattering
teeth, "just please let it be somewhere hot!"

The god of the Underworld, with his
human body and jackal's
head, rose up.

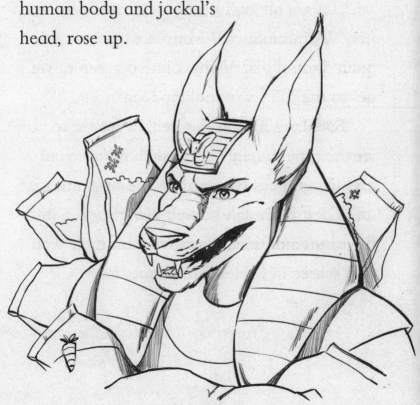

His furry face sparkled with frost and his red eyes glowed hot, melting all the frost and ice in an instant. He let out a long, low growl.

"A-Anubis," Isis said. "Nice of you to drop by."

"Are you ready to begin your next adventure?" Anubis shouted.

"But we haven't been up the sweets aisle yet," Tom moaned. "Mum always lets me open a family-sized chocolate bar before we get to the till. I was looking forward to it!"

"Silence!" Anubis shouted. "Prepare to leave immediately!" A tornado of icy wind and frozen peas whipped up round Tom, Isis and Cleo. Tom felt himself being sucked into the tunnels of time. They were on their way to a whole new place and era.

CHAPTER 2
THE GREEK ARMY

Tom, Isis and Cleo shot out of the time
tunnel. They floated down, down, down…
it was as if they had jumped out of an
aeroplane wearing invisible parachutes.

I love this bit, Tom thought.

The air that whooshed past his cheeks was
hot. Through barely open eyelids, Tom spied
the ground below rushing up to meet them.

Thump! Flump! Kerplump! The three
travellers landed on something hot and soft.

Tom sat up. The sunlight was blinding. The heat was fierce. Their last two time-travelling adventures had taken them to cold places – King Arthur's medieval England and Scandinavia in Viking times.

"Where are we?" he asked, shielding his blue eyes from the glare. The fingers on his left hand pushed down into powdery white sand. He and Isis were both wearing short tunics and sandals.

"I don't know, but it's glorious!" Isis said, leaping to her feet and jumping up and down with glee. "It's the first time I've been warm since we went to Ancient Rome!" She stretched out her arms and kissed the bronze skin that now covered them. "Hello, body! So nice to have you back."

Cleo mewed loudly and rubbed up against Isis's legs. She was covered in the furry stripes of a tabby cat once more.

"We need clues," Tom said.

He looked round. To his right, as far as he could see, were pale stone walls reaching up to the blue sky. To his left, the green sea was fringed by dazzlingly white sand. The beach was teaming with…

"Soldiers!" Isis cried.

Tom held his hand over her mouth and dragged her behind a sand dune. "Shh!" he said. "Not so loud. Let's work out who these guys are before—"

"First of all," Isis scoffed, "it's my job to talk loudly. I'm a princess! Second of all, they might be able to tell us where my amulet is."

Tom squinted at the soldiers' uniforms. On top of bright red tunics they wore bronze breastplates that made them look as though they had rippling muscles. On their legs, they

wore sandals with straps that held metal shin
pads in place. They carried round shields
with pictures on the front – some showed
winged horses and some had the letter V
upside down. But best of all...

"See those plumed helmets?" Tom said.
"I've seen those in Dad's museum. They're
Ancient Greek army helmets. And that upside-
down V was the symbol of the Spartan army."
He peered up at the pale stone walls. "Those

look like the walls to some ancient city. But the Greeks are on the outside, so—"

"They've got lovely horses," Isis said. She climbed on to Tom's back for a better look. "Stallions!" she said. "And they're tied together in groups. I think these soldiers are getting ready for battle."

Tom nodded. He looked up at a tall wooden contraption that loomed high above the soldiers. It looked like a giant catapult made from enormous planks of wood, levers and ropes.

"What's that ugly thing?" Isis asked.

Tom racked his brains for the name. He had seen a diagram of one in his history books. "It's a trebuchet!" he said, suddenly remembering. "They plonk massive boulders into the hammock thingy on the end of the rope and catapult them against the city walls."

"The Greeks are planning an invasion,"
Isis said, stroking Cleo as she scanned the
beach. "So it's going to be chaos at any
moment. We'd better find out where to look
for Anubis's amulet quick!"

Isis looked down
at the magic gold
scarab-shaped ring
that she'd worn
throughout her
life. It had a
hieroglyph of her
namesake on it,
the goddess Isis.

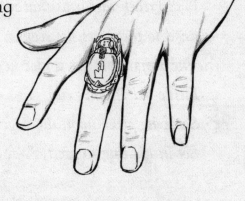

"Oh, lovely goddess Isis! Please, please,
pretty please, help us find the next amulet!"
she said.

The scarab ring began to make a whirring
noise... and silvery-coloured words flew out

of the ring and started to arrange themselves into lines. Soon the riddle was hanging complete in mid-air.

Tom read it aloud to Isis:

"The horse that roars a battle cry,
A wooden gift from the Greeks,
Will breach the walls that reach the sky,
Lead to the jewel she seeks.
The Trojan folk are under siege
Inside old Priam's city,
Seek the prize upon the liege!
Set in his ring so pretty."

"I've got it!" Tom said. "Or at least part of it."

Isis looked hopefully at him. "It sounds like a pile of nonsense. Go on. Explain it to me and Cleo."

Tom could just about contain his excitement. "Well, it mentions Trojans and Greeks and a horse. Have you heard of the Siege of Troy?" he asked.

Isis cocked her head to one side and frowned. "I've heard of Greece, obviously. But I can't remember much about Troy."

"Well, Troy was a really powerful nation too," Tom said. "About one thousand six hundred years after you died, the Greeks went to war with the Trojans. I'm pretty sure that's what the riddle's talking about."

Isis snorted. "Sounds like the Greeks were always waging war with someone. What were they fighting over?" She asked, stroking Cleo's silky fur.

Tom chuckled. "You'll love this! The different Greek armies sailed across the Aegean Sea with a massive fleet of ships...

and all because Helen left her husband, King Menelaus of Sparta – a city in Greece – to be with Prince Paris. He was the son of Priam, the king of Troy."

"They started a war over a girl?!" said Isis. She shook her head and laughed.

As Tom tightened his sandals' laces, he explained. "Helen was meant to be the most beautiful woman in the world. So when she left Menelaus, she broke his heart. Menelaus went bonkers and demanded that Paris give Helen back. But Paris wouldn't, so the Greeks declared war. Simple!"

"Egypt would never wage war over anything that silly," Isis said. "Mind you," she added thoughtfully, "*I* was the most gorgeous princess that Egypt had ever seen. If I'd been kidnapped, Father *definitely* would have sent his army after me!"

She started to stroke her plaits, and Tom noticed a dreamy look in her eyes. He clicked his fingers in front of her face.

"Wake up!" he said. "If you ever want to get into the Afterlife, we've got an amulet to find. And judging by the riddle, it's behind those city walls. We'd better start coming up with a plan to get inside, because the Trojans kept the Greeks out for *ten* years!"

Boink! Doink! Rattatatatat!

A strange banging noise interrupted Tom. He and Isis crept along the sand dunes until they came to a dense clump of fir trees. A band of workmen was hammering away at an enormous sculpture made from tree trunks. Some of them were arguing with a group of soldiers.

"Whatever is that thing?" Isis asked, pointing to the looming object.

Tom grinned with delight. "It's a horse. Can't you see? Legs, head, tail!" Tom had read about the legendary battle of Troy. Could this possibly be *the* wooden horse that had changed the course of the Trojan War?

Isis squinted at the pile of trunks. "*That's* a horse? The Greeks weren't very good with a hammer and chisel, were they? Not a patch on the Egyptians."

Before Tom could plan their next move, Isis and Cleo were strutting towards the craftsmen.

"You lot!" Isis shouted, hands on hips. "You've done the horse's legs far too short. And what's with the wheels? Horses don't have wheels! Can't you see that the head makes it look like a giant cow?"

The workmen turned round to face Isis with confused faces. They looked as though they hadn't understood her. But Tom knew that, thanks to Anubis's magic, everyone could understand them wherever they went.

One of the men stooped down and stared at Isis.

"A cow?!" he said. "It looks nothing like a cow! There must be something wrong with your eyes if you can't see that it's a horse. You got a fever, son?" He slapped a rough hand on to Isis's forehead.

Isis batted the man away. "Ugh! Leave me alone! What *is* this... thing?"

The man looked proudly up at the wooden horse. "This is an offering to the gods, of course!" he said. "The siege is going so badly, we thought we'd make something to tip things in our favour."

Suddenly, the squabbling soldiers rounded on Tom, Isis, Cleo and the workmen. Their

daggers were drawn and pointing right at them.

The ringleader picked out Isis. "The boy with the stupid hair is right," he growled. "If you lot had made the horse better, we might have broken down those walls by now!"

"I'm not a bo—" Isis began to protest.

Tom nudged her. "Shh! Don't let them know you're a girl," he whispered in Isis's ear. "We might need to pass ourselves off as soldiers."

Isis nodded and held her tongue.

Another angry soldier poked one of the workmen in the chest. He had a sweaty face and fierce, dark eyes. "It's your fault we're losing the war," he snarled.

The band of soldiers waved their fists in the air at the carpenters.

"We blame you!" they yelled.

"Get them, boys!" shouted the ringleader.

CHAPTER 3
THE LEGENDARY ODYSSEUS

There was a *swoosh* by Tom's ear as a sword cut through the air. Then a deafening *clang* as it clashed against a carpenter's saw.

"You have displeased the gods!" the sword-wielding soldier cried. "Your wooden cow is terrible."

"It's not a cow. It's a horse, you idiot!" the workman shouted, waving his saw. "We're going to win the war with that!"

The group of soldiers and workmen were

locked in a tussle that would have had Ares, the Greek god of war, in a spin.

No wonder they're losing the war, thought Tom. *They're too busy fighting each other.*

Tom looked for Isis and Cleo in the fray. Cleo was darting through the men's legs and digging her claws into their shins. But where was Isis?

"Let me through, you big, sweaty brutes!" Tom heard her cry.

Finally he caught sight of her, kicking out at the men as they rained punches down on each other.

"Isis!" Tom shouted, elbowing a soldier in the belly. "We've got to get out of here."

He held out his hand towards her. Isis was just about to take it when Tom spotted a tall, muscly carpenter holding a hammer above his head.

"Out of my way, Spartan child soldier!"

Tom squeezed his eyes shut and waited for the hammer to attack him. But the blow didn't come.

"Stop this fighting at once, you mules!" a commanding voice bellowed.

Tom opened his eyes to see his attacker being pushed to the ground by an older man. He wore a fine breastplate and a helmet topped with a red plume.

"Commanders! Come to my aid!" the man shouted.

As Tom and Isis finally managed to prise themselves free, three important-looking men ran out of a large red tent pitched nearby.

Tom could see the outside was decorated with the upside-down V symbol.

"Cool! These Spartan soldiers were really famous!" he whispered to Isis excitedly.

"What do you mean, 'cool'?" Isis asked. "Getting roped into a fight the minute we arrive is hardly a great start." She picked up Cleo and held her close to her chest. "We've got to get out of here."

"No!" Tom said. "Let's just see what happens. We might get some clues that will help us find the amulet. The riddle mentioned the wooden horse..."

Tom, Isis and Cleo watched as the

commanders dragged the soldiers away from the angry workmen.

The older commander took off his helmet and held it under his arm. His hair was short and grey. "You lot are making the Greek army look like fools," he said.

"What does it matter?" one of the soldiers said, holding his hand over what Tom could see was already turning into a whopping black eye. "The Trojans have been laughing at us behind their unbreakable walls for years. We've tried everything we can think of to get inside that city. This siege is a joke!"

The commander pushed the soldier roughly towards the entrance of the tent. He turned to the rest of the bruised and sorry-looking rabble.

"You think that's an excuse to start

fighting amongst yourselves?" he shouted.
"Well! You idiots can explain yourselves to
the Chief Commander Odysseus himself."

The commander held a flap to one side.
Tom stood on his tiptoes to get a look inside
the tent.

"Can you believe it?" he asked Isis.
"We're going to meet Odysseus! He was
an amazing warrior. He commanded all
the different Greek armies, including the
Spartans."

Isis sniffed and examined her fingernails.
"If they haven't been able to break into Troy
in ten years, he can't be that amazing."

One by one, the soldiers entered the tent
to speak to Odysseus. Soon it was Tom and
Isis's turn.

"Get in there!" the grey-haired
commander said.

He pushed them both inside the tent, which was now crowded with burly soldiers, who looked like they had just been given a telling-off.

With a pounding heart, Tom scanned the tent. In the middle a young, dark-haired man was sitting in a chair that was far too big for him. He was wearing a gold breastplate clearly meant for someone with rippling biceps and a broad chest. *That's the legendary Odysseus?* thought Tom. *He looks like a kid wearing his dad's armour!*

Odysseus crossed his skinny legs and swished a tasselled fly swatter in Tom's and Isis's direction but accidentally swatted himself on the nose. He blushed.

"You two children! Come forward!" he said in a whiny voice that reminded Tom of his teacher, Mr Braintree, when he had a cold. "Which army are you from?" demanded Odysseus.

Tom and Isis shuffled towards the chair.

"Please, Mr Odysseus," Tom said. "We've only just got here. We never meant to get roped into a fight."

Odysseus looked them up and down. "You're too young to be Agamemnon's soldiers," he said. "And I know all of Achilles's warriors." He stood, stepped forward and grasped Tom's face in his hands. "You must be Spartans sent by Menelaus! Only Spartans force cubs to fight like bears."

"Yes," Isis said, smiling. "That's *exactly* what we are! Deadly bear cubs. Grrrr!"

Odysseus strode to the back of the tent. As he passed a small table stacked with drinks, he knocked the edge of the tabletop with his enormous breastplate. The table wobbled from side to side.

"Er, Odysseus, sir," the grey-haired commander said, slapping his hand to his forehead. "Watch the—"

But it was too late. The table fell sideways and the cups rolled on to the floor with a clatter. Odysseus seemed not to have noticed. He simply snatched up two helmets from a pile and tossed them to Tom and Isis. His throw was so bad that Tom had to leap to the side to catch his. Isis's helmet landed in the sand a metre away from her.

"You Spartan shrimps must get yourselves kitted out with some armour." He turned to the crowd of soldiers that stood in glum silence, staring down at their sandals. "Now listen up, you lot! We're about to begin a new attack on the walls of Troy. And as punishment for being troublemakers, you'll be leading the charge."

Odysseus rubbed his hands together and grinned. The soldiers started to complain loudly.

"But that means we'll be the first to get killed!" one soldier said.

"Well, you should have thought of that before you attacked the carpenters!" Odysseus replied.

The grey-haired commander, who was much taller than Odysseus, stepped forward and bowed.

"Yes, Commander Leandros. Speak!" Odysseus said, sounding annoyed.

"What is your plan of attack, sir? Shall these men prepare to fight immediately?" he asked.

Tom looked at Isis and gulped. *On our other adventures, we've had time to get to know a few people and work out a plan*, Tom thought.

But we're just going to get thrown in the deep end here! He was sure Isis was thinking the same thing as she chewed nervously on her bottom lip.

Odysseus strode back to his chair and promptly tripped over his own feet. He sat down heavily and tapped his head. "I'm still perfecting the plan. It's all up here."

Isis snorted loudly.

Tom nudged her. "He hasn't got a clue, has he?" he whispered. "But he needs to get us inside that city and I know *exactly* how he should do it!"

Tom knew that someone would come up with the plan eventually, but he and Isis didn't have any time to lose. He decided to give history a helping hand.

As the soldiers filed out of the tent, Tom took a deep breath and approached Odysseus.

"Er, excuse me, Mr Odysseus," he said, hoping the disappointing legend would not smack him in the face with his fly swatter. "I've got an idea."

Odysseus leaned forward. "What is it, boy?" he asked impatiently.

"Well, you know that brilliant wooden horse outside?" Tom said.

Odysseus nodded. "My idea!" he said.

"Um… have you thought about offering it to the Trojans as a gift?" Tom asked. He remembered all the details from books he'd read about the Trojan War.

"A gift?!" Odysseus threw back his head and wheezed with laughter. "What a ridiculous idea. Why would I waste such a splendid thing on our enemies?"

Tom sighed. "I mean, you could fill the horse with soldiers, leave it outside the gates,

move all your ships out of sight, as though you've given up and set sail for Greece... Who knows? Maybe they'll wheel it inside, and then, *bam!* You can spring a surprise attack and take the city."

Odysseus stopped chuckling. Tom was sure he could hear the cogs creaking as they turned inside his head, working through the details of Tom's suggestion with painful slowness.

"If it works, you'd be a hero," Tom said.

"Hmm," Odysseus said, scratching his cheek with his fly swatter.

He suddenly sprang out of his chair.

"Listen up!" he shouted to his commanders. "I have had the most amazing idea!"

CHAPTER 4
A GIFTED HORSE

Tom was climbing a rope attached to a fir tree branch. He looked down at the sandy ground and saw a sea of faces frowning up at him as the group of soldiers waited to take their turn.

As he gripped the scratchy rope, Tom's hands stung. He took a deep breath and pulled himself up as hard as he could. One of the soldiers approached the foot of the tree.

"Get on with it, little Spartan!" he shouted.

"Odysseus wants us *all* to be perfect at getting in and out of that horse by sunset. But you're hogging the practice tree!"

"I'm doing my best, OK?" Tom called down. Then he muttered to himself, "Come on, Tom, one hand over the other, like in gym."

Finally, he reached the top and hauled himself on to the branch.

Glancing down, Tom could see the carpenters working hard to rebuild the wooden horse. A pile of wood shavings had

grown under the horse's massive belly. It looked like a giant heap of grated cheese. Tom smiled. Odysseus had ordered the carpenters to prepare the hiding place inside the horse as though it had been his idea and not Tom's.

Who'd have thought I would give history a nudge in the right direction? Tom thought. *That's the most amazing thing ever!*

"Er... HELLO!" Isis shouted up at him.
"You have to come down, once you've
reached the top!"

Tom chuckled and carefully slid down
the rope to the ground.

"Easy!" he said, breathing out deeply
when his feet hit the sand.

Isis snorted. "Easy? I'll show you easy!
Watch this!" she said.

The princess started to shin up the tree,
but she was clearly struggling as much as
Tom had.

"Easy-peasy, isn't it?" Tom said, grinning.

"Ugh!" Isis grunted. "This rope is too
slippery!"

"One hand over the other!" Tom called
up helpfully.

Only Cleo had no problem with the climb.
She mewed loudly and scampered up after

her mistress, digging her sharp claws into the fat rope. But once she got to the top she yowled with fright. Tom could see her little furry body shaking with fear as she clung to the branch.

Grey-haired Commander Leandros marched to the foot of the tree and looked up at Cleo. His hawk-like features had bunched up into a scowl. Tom could tell he was not amused.

"Get that fleabag out of here!" he shouted at Isis. "NOW!"

Rolling her eyes, Isis slid down, holding Cleo. She cuddled the quivering cat close to her chest. "Take no notice of the nasty man, my little furry love," she said to her cat.

Tom pulled Isis to one side. "Look," he said. "You're not going to be able to take Cleo in the horse. There's no way that

Commander Leandros will allow it."

Isis gasped. "I am NOT going anywhere without my FLUFFPOT!" she said, poking Tom in the shoulder. Her eyes flashed and her fists were balled tight. "If you think for one minute—"

Tom shook his head. He could feel frustration bubbling away inside him. "Isis! Think about it! This horse is our first-class ticket into Troy. Once we're inside, all we have to do is find King Priam and get the amulet!" He tried to choose his words carefully. "It's like when we were in Ancient Rome and Cleo stayed with the other animals while we were training to be gladiators... if you can find a safe hiding place for her—"

Isis stamped her foot in the sand. "No, no, NO!"

Clasping his hands to his head, Tom groaned. Then, as he watched a carpenter bagging wood shavings into a rough, grey sack, a thought struck him.

"We'll put her in a sack!" he said. "You can carry it slung over your shoulder. Hopefully, nobody will notice."

Cleo purred and twitched her whiskers. She offered Tom a velvety paw.

"Even Cleo thinks that's a good idea," he said.

Isis nodded curtly. "Oh, all right then. Better than leaving her behind, I suppose."

Suddenly they were interrupted by somebody clapping.

"Gather round, men!"

Tom turned to see Odysseus standing at the foot of the fir tree. He was holding the rope and looking very pleased with himself.

The soldiers drew closer.

"Now we need to be quick and confident in our ambush of Troy," he told the soldiers. "That's why I came up with the excellent idea of practising climbing up and down this rope."

Tom saw that the soldiers were looking at Odysseus with glazed eyes. Some were sniggering behind their hands. Odysseus seemed not to notice.

"As your leader, I'm going to give you a demonstration of how it should be done!"

Odysseus grabbed the rope and tugged on it. The soldiers were nudging each other and winking now. The legendary commander climbed up about three metres, then he yelped and slid down, landing in the sand on his bottom! His cheeks were flame red.

"Anyway," Odysseus said, dusting himself

off and kicking the trunk, "the wooden horse is ready now. Prepare to hide yourselves inside. We will put my plan of great cunning into operation tonight!"

Under the hot afternoon sun, the Greek army packed away its camp. Everything they had brought, including the giant trebuchet, was carried back on to the fleet of ships, which were moored some way off the beach.

Tom stared at the hundreds of vessels, bobbing on the glittering sea. "I love those Greek ships," he said to Isis. "Have you seen the eyes on each side of the front? Mega cool!"

"Those little tubs aren't as impressive as my father's barges," Isis scoffed. She pulled out a sack from under her tunic. "Look! I swiped one of these. Let's get Cleo inside."

Cleo started to hiss and scratch as Tom
gripped her wriggling body. He lifted her
towards the sack that Isis held open.

"MEOW! YEOUW! WOOOW!" Cleo
drew her claws across his arm,
making red stripes.

"Ow!" Tom cried.

"Get in the sack, Cleo! It's either that or you get left behind with the rest of the Greek soldiers. They're all setting sail for the next bay along. Do you fancy getting wet?"

"I think Fluffpot had more than enough of sailing when we went to sea with the Vikings," Isis said, laughing.

Yowling and flailing her paws around, Cleo finally allowed herself to be put inside the sack. Isis arranged it carefully across her body.

Odysseus called the squad of soldiers to take their places. One by one, the men clambered up the rope that dangled from underneath the huge wooden horse and climbed inside.

"It's time," Isis said, running towards the rope. She hoisted herself up and through the trapdoor.

Only Tom was left. He looked up into the darkness of the horse's belly. It was like a giant wooden cave. Isis, peering out of the hiding place, shouted, "Come on!"

Commander Leandros leaned out of the hatch and called down. "Are you coming, Spartan?" he asked, holding out his hand. "Or shall we leave you to take on the might of the Trojans by yourself?"

Tom grabbed the rope and started to climb. As he dangled in the air, he took one last look at the beach. It was sparkling white. There was no trace that the Greek army had had so much as a picnic, let alone camped there for ten years. His heart hammered inside his chest. The moment of truth was upon them. Would the Trojans really fall for the wooden-horse trick?

CHAPTER 5
LETTING THE CAT OUT OF THE BAG

"Move up, you big buffoon!" Isis said to one of the men crouching next to her. "You're standing on my toes."

"Move where, exactly?" the soldier answered. "Shall I sit on your shoulders instead?"

Tom ran his fingers through his sweaty hair. The body heat from the soldiers squashed on either side of him made him feel like he was being blasted by a furnace.

The only light in the belly of the horse came from the slight gap around the trapdoor by his feet. He could just about make out Isis as she elbowed the stocky soldier so hard that he toppled on to the man next to him.

"Chief Commander, sir!" the soldier complained to Odysseus. "Do I have your permission to beat this little Spartan? He just pushed me over."

Odysseus's muffled voice replied, "Behave yourselves!"

A noise ripped through the darkness.

"Aw, Demodocus has just let one go, boss," another man complained.

Everyone inside the horse groaned as the smell of rotten eggs wafted round the cramped space.

"He who smelt it, dealt it!" a deep voice barked.

"Shut up, Demodocus. Everybody knows it's you!"

"Men! Hold your tongues now!" ordered Odysseus. But no one was listening to him.

"Move up, you bunch of stinkers. I've got cramp in my calf."

"Ow! Eugenius shoved his stinky foot on my—"

"SILENCE!" came the voice of Commander Leandros.

Everybody instantly hushed.

Tom felt his bones judder and heard the wooden wheels squeaking as the Spartan soldiers rolled the wooden horse over the uneven ground beneath them. When the horse ground to a halt, Tom knew the horse was in position outside the city gates, as planned. He imagined the walls of Troy looming above them.

★

It felt like hours had passed, but sitting there in the dark Tom had no way of knowing how much time had actually gone by. Every moment seemed to drag as they waited nervously inside the wooden horse, and Tom got pins and needles in his feet from standing still for so long.

Atishoooo! Suddenly the sweaty silence was torn apart by a sneeze.

"Eeuw, I felt that on the back of my neck!" came a voice in the gloom.

Then... *Achoooooo!*

Isis shrieked. "It's raining snot!" she cried.

Tom squinted in the murk to see who was responsible. There, just by Isis's shoulder, was Odysseus. He was wiping his nose on his tunic. Stretching his skinny arms out wide, he started to grope everyone he could reach.

"Who's wearing fur?" he asked. "Out with it! I know one of you is... is... *IS... ACHOOO! ATISHOO! WHAAAHOO!*" There was no let-up, as Odysseus sprayed the soldiers with snot again and again and again.

The soldier who was crouched next to Isis held his shield over his head like an umbrella. "No, boss," he said. "Everyone here knows that fur makes you sneeze like the gods themselves have cursed you."

A legendary Greek warrior with a terrible fur allergy. And a fluffy cat in an enclosed space. Whoops, thought Tom.

"All of you! Reach out to your right and have a good feel," Commander Leandros said. "We must find out who is wearing fur!"

In the dim light, Tom saw Isis's eyes widen with horror. She snatched the sack away from her neighbour's reach. Suddenly Cleo mewed.

"There's a cat in here!" Odysseus spluttered, sounding as though he had a bag of marbles stuffed up each nostril.

"No," Isis said. "It was my tummy rumbling." Isis started to make a groaning noise.

Just as Odysseus was about to grab Isis by the shoulder, an almighty creaking noise stopped him. The whole wooden horse had started to shake.

"The gates are being opened!" Isis whispered.

Tom held his breath. There was not a single trump or burp or sneeze to be heard now. The soldiers inside the wooden horse strained to listen to the gatekeepers.

Beneath the trapdoor, Tom could hear the scuffling of sandals in the sand.

"What do you think to that then, Aeneas?" one man said.

There was a belch. Then a sniff. "Dunno. Who ever heard of a wooden cow being left at the gates of Troy?"

"Do you think it's a cow? Looks like a giant goat to me. Or a horse, maybe. Go and fetch Heroditus. He's a clever fellow. He'll know what to make of this."

More and more men seemed to gather beneath the horse. Tom wondered whether

71

they could hear the thumping of his heart in his chest. Across from him, he could see Odysseus holding his hand to his face, desperately trying to stifle another sneeze.

The hubbub from the excited Trojans beneath them suddenly fell silent.

"Here he is! Go on, Heroditus!" said the first man who had spoken. "Tell us what you make of it."

"Why! This is a gift to the gods from the Greeks," Heroditus said in a hearty voice.

"A gift? Yes! A gift!" called out several voices.

Everybody seemed to be listening to Heroditus, as though he was in charge.

"It is an apology from the Greeks, for them spending ten years trying to break down our mighty city walls," Heroditus said. "It is a fitting tribute. Wheel it inside, men!"

But amongst the babble of general agreement, Tom heard the croaking voice of what sounded like an elderly man.

"It's a trap, I tell you!"

"Oh, be quiet, you old fool."

The trembling voice started up again. "Beware gifts from the Greeks!"

Isis clasped her hand to her forehead. Some of the soldiers breathed in sharply, their shoulders hunched up near their ears.

Is this it? Tom thought, waiting to be discovered. *We get to the gates and we're turned away? No ambush? No amulet!*

A fist rapped on the underside of the horse. "Seems solid enough to me," Aeneas said. "Ignore the old misery guts there. Wheel it in, men!"

Inside the belly of the horse, some of the soldiers thrust up their thumbs through the fingers of their clenched fists and punched the air. Tom remembered from his history books that this was an Ancient Greek way of wishing each other good luck. He couldn't help but join in. Suddenly it didn't feel as gloomy in there as it had before.

The wooden horse started to rumble and shake again as the Trojans pushed the giant gift into the city. Tom heard the gates clang shut behind them.

"We're in!" he whispered to Isis. "Now all we have to do is find the amulet and go home!"

CHAPTER 6
AN UNWANTED GIFT

"Right men, *ATISHOO!*" Odysseus finally whispered. "The sun has been down for a good while. It's time to spring our attack!"

Tom marvelled that the Trojans had not discovered the Greek soldiers, hidden away in the belly of the horse. But judging by the shouting and singing that had been going on outside for hours, the Trojans had been too busy celebrating the Greeks' departure to hear Odysseus's constant sneezing. Now though, the sound of merriment had faded.

The Greek soldiers shifted about in the blackness. They grunted and groaned. Pins and needles jabbed at Tom, as the life started to flow slowly back into his arms and legs.

"On the count of three, pull the trapdoor up!" Odysseus said quietly. "One... *ACHOOO*... two!"

Tom's heart started to gallop. There was a rattle as the soldiers round him gathered up their weapons. Tom found himself wishing that he and Isis had swords of their own.

"Three!"

In almost perfect silence, the trapdoor was lifted up. Cool night air and the salty smell of the sea wafted up into the crowded wooden horse. All was silent below. The

first few soldiers swung
down on the rope. Tom
quickly followed, then
Isis. They hit the ground
with a dull thud and
looked about.

They were in a large, paved square, dimly lit by flaming torches and surrounded by buildings. In the centre of the square, close to the wooden horse, was an enormous, gurgling fountain. Long black shadows covered the ground like giant slugs.

"What are those?" Tom whispered. He squinted in the flickering firelight. The shadows were snoring. "Sleeping soldiers!"

Isis yelped and grabbed Tom's arm.

"Aargh!" cried Tom.

Standing only moments away from where he and Isis had landed, Tom saw a gang of Trojan soldiers. They were swaying slightly and seemed to be propping each other up. In their hands, they held jugs of wine. Open-mouthed and bleary-eyed, they stared up at the trapdoor, watching in silence as the Greeks dropped out of the horse's belly.

79

The silence didn't last for long.

"Attack! Attack!" the Trojan soldiers cried. "Raise the alarm! Seize your weapons!"

The Trojan soldiers charged towards the Greeks, with deadly looking spears outstretched.

"We've got to get out of here!" Isis shouted.

She skipped nimbly over a snoring Trojan and hid behind a column. "But first I must let poor Fluffpot out of this horrible bag," she said, loosening the drawstrings.

With a delighted yowl, Cleo leaped out of the sack. She stretched and twitched her whiskers, then strutted off. After a short distance she turned to meow at Tom and Isis.

"I think she wants us to follow her," Tom said. He looked back to see three Trojans running towards them with their daggers drawn.

"Run!" Isis shouted.

Cleo sprang away towards the far side of the square. Tom and Isis followed, hurdling drunken Trojans and dodging Greek arrows meant for the startled city guards.

Pretty soon they found themselves sprinting down dingy, narrow alleys, lit only by the glow of the full moon.

Tom peered up at crumbling buildings. The narrow windows seemed to be watching him. Ragged, grotty clothes hung from the window ledges.

Cleo slowed down. She padded past battered-looking doors and rubbish-strewn steps. A deep gutter carried stinky black liquid down the length of the alley.

Isis wrinkled her nose in the moonlight. "It's kind of grotty round here," she said.

"What do you expect, Princess?" Tom said. "They've been under siege for the past ten years!" He stopped and stood still. "Listen!"

Isis held her hand to one ear. The only sound was the distant crashing of the sea against the shore. "I don't hear anything," she said, frowning.

"Exactly!" Tom exclaimed. "No fighting!"

Isis grinned at her pet in the silvery moonlight. "Clever Cleo brought us to a safe part of the city."

Walking a little further, they came across a deep hole set into the thick city wall.

"I'm pretty sure this is some kind of alcove," Tom said, looking at the hiding place. "If you're tired, we can sit here and rest a minute."

"Tired? Pah! Not a chance!" Isis said, still panting after their sprint. "Don't blame *me* if you need to rest your wimpy boy bones. I'm going to keep going and find King Priam."

Tom ignored her and removed his helmet. "If we're going to survive, we'd better start looking like Trojans. Take off your helmet."

"All right! Stop bossing me around, Professor Smartypants."

As Isis tugged her plaits free of her plumed Greek army helmet, Tom heard footsteps approaching. He pulled Isis and Cleo into the shadows of the alcove. A boy tottered into view. He was carrying a huge pile of logs that looked far too heavy for him. Despite that, he was whistling a merry tune.

"Do you think he's dangerous?" Isis asked. "Could he be a spy?"

"Don't be ridiculous! He's just a kid," Tom whispered to Isis. "Maybe he can help us."

Tom jumped out of the alcove so suddenly that the boy dropped some of his logs with a clatter.

"Hello there!" Tom said in a friendly voice. He tried to think of the sort of thing his dad would say to a stranger he'd just met. "Nice evening, isn't it!"

The boy looked at Tom and frowned. Then he glanced up at the moon and shrugged. "Yes, I suppose it is," he said. "I'm Hermon. I haven't seen you round here before. Who are you?"

Tom stooped to gather up the fallen wood. "I'm Tom. This is Isis," he said, pointing to Isis, who was stroking Cleo. "We were out for a walk and got lost. Where are you heading with this heavy load?"

Hermon wedged the tall pile of wood underneath his chin. "I'm just taking some firewood to the palace," he said. "That near where you want to go?"

Tom looked over at Isis, who suddenly sat bolt upright. "Priam's palace?" Tom asked.

Hermon chuckled. "The one and only."

Isis bounded over to them. She grabbed some of Hermon's logs. "Let us help carry these. We'll walk with you to the palace," Isis said, looking sideways at Tom and winking.

Hermon shovelled a pile of logs into her arms until Isis started to buckle at the knees.

"Hang on! I said I'd help!" she grumbled. "I didn't say I'd take *all* of them."

Tom stuffed a pile of wood under his arm. "Thanks, Hermon. I think Priam's palace might be just the direction we need to head towards!"

Together, Tom, Isis, Cleo and Hermon trudged through the moonlit warren of alleys and silent squares. Isis told Hermon a story about having travelled from Egypt to visit her uncle, a trader who had sailed across the sea, selling exotic goods, until he met a Trojan woman and settled down. The story was so convincing, even Tom started to believe it!

Finally they ambled down an olive tree-lined road that led to the back of the palace.

"If you don't mind helping me into the servants' quarters with these," Hermon said, "I can probably sort you out with some goat's milk and bread for your trouble."

Tom couldn't believe their luck. He nodded vigorously. "You bet," he said. "Let's go."

Hermon led them into the hustle and bustle of the palace kitchens. Even at that late hour, servants darted to and fro, preparing food by the light of flaming torches. But just as Tom and Isis piled their logs next to the fire in the centre of the room, the sound of angry men's voices started to bounce off the stone walls. Tom strained to hear where the sound was coming from.

"I'm going to burn this palace down, and everyone in it!" one of the men bellowed.

Were they Greek soldiers? Tom wondered in alarm. Oh no! How would they ever find the amulet if the palace was under attack?

CHAPTER 7
ALL FIRED UP

"Let's run away before we get burned to a crisp!" Tom yelped.

Isis snatched up Cleo. "Quick! Where can we hide?" she asked Hermon.

Hermon chuckled and shrugged. "Hide? You're kidding, aren't you? They always argue like that."

Tom frowned. He breathed deeply, willing his heartbeat to slow down. "What? Who?"

"King Priam and his son, Paris," Hermon

said. "The king blames Paris for starting the war with the Greeks because he stole Helen from Menelaus of Sparta. Don't worry. Nobody's going to burn the palace down." Hermon wiped his hands on his tunic.

"Imagine that! King Priam's just down that corridor!" Tom said, blinking hard as he stared into the gloom beyond the kitchen.

Hermon nodded. "Yes. That's right. It's not that exciting, though." He pointed to a stool by the wall. "Sit there out of the way. I'll get you something to eat."

Isis dashed over to the stool and sat down. Tom pinned himself to the wall, keeping out of the way of the servants who scurried past, carrying platters of food and jugs of wine.

"No one here knows about the attack yet, do they?" he whispered to Isis.

"No," she said. "This could be our only

chance to get close to Priam. We just need a plan…"

As they waited for Hermon to return with their bread and milk, Tom looked about the kitchen, racking his brain for a bright idea that would get them into the royal quarters.

"I'm hungry!" Isis complained. "Where's Hermon with my snack?"

"Shh. I'm trying to think," Tom said. But the smell of food was distracting.

In the centre of the room, lamb was turning on a spit and roasting over the open fire. The greasy smoke wafted straight up through a hole in the ceiling. Tom sniffed the air and breathed in the smell of stewing vegetables. Women were straining watery white cheese through muslin cloths. A male servant was arranging figs, olives and grapes on a large silver platter.

"Oh, it's no use!" Tom said, sighing. "It's hours and hours since we ate anything. I just can't concentrate." His mouth started to water.

All the while, a grumpy-looking young man was barking instructions at the many servants. Those who didn't do as he said quickly enough were hit on the head with a wooden spoon.

"What a monster!" Isis said.

Hermon returned with four pieces of flatbread, some white, crumbly goat's cheese that smelled like socks, and a jug of goat's milk. "Oh, talking about Phineus, are you?" he asked, setting a bowl of milk on the floor for Cleo. "He's the boss here. Don't let him catch you hanging about. Or you'll get The Spoon!"

Tom and Isis both bit hungrily into their breads. They watched as Phineus prodded the meat on the spit with a fork.

Suddenly a mouse darted across the kitchen floor. Cleo's ears immediately flattened against the side of her furry head. With a hungry yowl, she streaked after the mouse as it scurried between Phineus's feet.

"Aargh!" Phineus cried.

He jumped, dropping the spit from the sticks that held it up over the fire. The hot, greasy lamb hissed as it hit the flaming logs below. Tom watched in horror as the lamb then fell on to Phineus's thigh. There was a nasty sizzling noise.

"Aaaaargh! Get it off me!" Phineus screamed.

Hermon rushed over to Phineus. With a cloth wrapped round his hand, he tossed the lamb to one side. Tom winced as he looked at Phineus's leg. The skin was bright red and shiny.

"You need to put ice on that," Tom suggested.

"Ice?" Hermon asked. "What on earth is ice? What this needs is a wet rag."

Hermon soaked a length of cloth in a bucket of water and wound it tightly round Phineus's burn. Phineus slapped him away.

"Get off! You're hurting me!" he shrieked.

Just as Hermon was knotting the end of the bandage, a voice boomed round the kitchen. It sounded like it was coming from the same corridor that King Priam and Paris had been arguing in.

"Bring us wine! Bring it now, boy!"

Phineus's face paled.

"You can't go in there with a burn like that," Hermon said.

"But it's Prince Paris!" Phineus gasped. He clutched at his burned thigh and swallowed hard. A sweat had broken out on his forehead. "I'm his servant. He'll have me flogged if I don't take in the tray."

Feeling excitement prickle his skin, Tom grabbed a wine jug and two shallow bowls. "Is this what you were going to take them?" he asked.

Phineus nodded.

Isis snatched up a silver platter and held it out so that Tom could load the jug and bowls on to it.

"We'll take it for you," she said.

Hermon pointed into the shadows. "Thanks! The throne room is the third door on the right. Hurry!"

Tom and Isis rushed along the dimly lit stone corridor, with Cleo scampering at their side. Tom was feeling nervous at the thought of meeting Paris and the king.

"Right," Tom said, thinking fast. "The riddle said that the amulet is in King Priam's ring. Maybe if we get close enough, we can cause a distraction and slip it off?"

Isis nodded. "Leave it to me," she said.

They reached large, carved double doors that had gold symbols painted all over them.

Two guards with stern faces stood on either side, holding spears in their hands.

As Tom offered the tray for them to inspect, angry voices erupted from the room beyond.

"You are past it, Father!" a young man shouted. "That's your trouble. The kingdom would be better off without you."

Tom pushed open the door, wondering what to expect. His heart thumped hard against his chest. Nobody seemed to noticed him and Isis enter.

As they glimpsed the terrible scene, Tom almost dropped the tray. An old man – King Priam, Tom assumed – was standing by the window. Behind him stood a tall young man. Tom guessed he was Prince Paris.

Paris's face was twisted in rage. He gripped the old man around the neck with

two strong hands. The king started to sink
to his knees with wide, terrified eyes. He
suddenly noticed Tom and held out his hand.

"Help me!" he gasped.

CHAPTER 8
THE KING'S RING

"Noooo!" Tom shouted. "Let the king go!"

Noticing the two children, Paris quickly let go of his father. The old king rubbed at his throat.

"You were strangling your own father!" Tom said, pointing an accusing finger at Paris.

Paris suddenly wore the same expression that Tom's dad had when Mum found him rummaging in the biscuit tin.

"Strangling the king?" he said, his eyes

darting about. "I was doing nothing of the sort!" He looked round the throne room, as though he was searching for a suitable excuse. Then he clapped his hands and laughed. "I was hugging him!" Paris gave his startled father a hug, a fake smile plastered on his face. "See!"

"Liar!" Isis shouted.

"Silence, servant!" Paris barked, his cheeks red with anger. He sprinted over to her with his hand raised. "I'm going to flog you, you cheeky little rat!" he shouted.

Isis's fists were balled. Cleo stuck out her claws and hissed.

"Call yourself royal, do you?" Isis shouted to Paris. "Well, come on, then! I'll show you how we deal with liars in Egypt!"

Tom couldn't work out who looked the more dangerous of the two. What Isis lacked

101

in height, she more than made up for in pluck. But Paris was tall and bulging with muscles.

"Enough!" the king croaked. "Paris! Be still, boy! Your quarrel is with me, not with this strange little servant." He looked at Isis and patted her head. He gave her a kindly smile. "Where do we find them these days? Egypt indeed! Most peculiar!"

The king shuffled over to his golden throne and grunted as he lowered himself on to it. Clutching his embroidered cloak round his stooped shoulders, he looked at the prince with tired, sad eyes.

"Come over here and sit by me, Paris," the king croaked, patting the chair at his right side with a wrinkled hand.

Tom thought he seemed neither angry at, nor scared of, his son.

Paris strode over to the throne. He sat

stiffly next to his father. When the king reached out to take his hand, Paris snatched it away.

"Come, son," the king said. "We should be united. For the good of Troy. This fighting serves no useful purpose. Let's drink to peace."

Priam turned to Tom and Isis. "Bring the drink here, now!"

Tom approached the throne slowly. The jug and two wine bowls rattled on the tray that he was carrying. He set them on to the low table that Isis had placed in front of Priam and Paris.

Suddenly, Tom's eye caught sight of the huge golden ring that Priam was wearing on his right hand. In the centre of the ring was a glittering, yellow jewel, like a shiny egg. The amulet!

Isis jabbed her finger towards it and cleared her throat. Tom nodded. This was it! But how could they get it off without Priam noticing?

Priam held out his bowl. "Pour! Pour!" he ordered Isis.

Isis held up the jug. She winked at Tom. Then she started to pour as much wine over King Priam's hand as she did in the bowl.

"You fool!" he shouted, flicking the drops of wine off his fingers and on to the floor.

Isis tore a strip from the hem of her tunic and began wiping the king's hand.

"Oooh, so sorry, Your Royal Highness. Dear, oh dear! I'm so clumsy!" she said.

Tom watched Isis slide the ring quickly off Priam's hand. She shoved it into her pocket.

"There, there!" she said. "All dry now."

She bowed low and grabbed Tom by the elbow.

"Quick!" she said out of the corner of her mouth.

Together, they edged backwards, towards the corridor where Cleo was waiting.

The heavy doors swung shut behind them.

"We've done it!" Isis whispered. She reached down and gave Cleo a cuddle.

Now all Tom, Isis and Cleo had to do was touch the amulet, and they'd be whisked back to where they had come from. But Cleo had her own ideas. She sniffed the air and started to pad back towards the bright lights of the kitchen, following the scent of roasted meat.

"Come back here, you silly cat," Tom hissed after Cleo.

Isis glared at Tom. "That's no way to talk to a royal cat! She's hungry."

"Pardon me for wanting to get out of here alive," Tom said. "How long do you think it will take Priam to notice that you've taken the amulet?"

Isis didn't need to reply. Just then an almighty roar echoed down the corridor. "That servant has stolen my ring!" shouted the king.

"Uh oh," said Tom. "Now we're in trouble."

"Let's get out of here, fast!" said Isis. "Run, Fluffpot!"

Tom and Isis ran down the corridor after the cat. They were chased by two royal guards carrying sharp spears. Behind them, Tom heard the heavy footsteps of a third man. He glanced behind. It was Paris! And he was gaining on them.

Cleo meowed and shot into the kitchen.

Tom glanced over his shoulder. The guards would be on them any moment.

"Let's just go!" he urged Isis. "Cleo will be happy here, hunting for mice."

"We can't go without Cleo!" Isis cried, as they ran into the kitchen.

Before Isis could scoop up her cat, the stones beneath their feet started to tremble. Tom and Isis slammed into one another, as crumbling rock spurted out of the ground in front of them.

Looking terrified, Cleo yowled and jumped out of a small window.

"Let me guess," Isis groaned. "Anubis!"

Sure enough, up popped the towering form of the Egyptian god of the Underworld himself. He stood between them and the window, blocking their way out. In his hand he held a huge jug.

"You're a *slippery* little pair, aren't you?" Anubis said, his deep voice rumbling round the kitchen. His red eyes shone with menace. "Let's see if you can get to grips with this!"

Anubis poured the contents of the jug on the floor. He threw back his head in a fit of nasty laughter, so that his fangs shone dangerously in the candlelight. In a flash of lightening, he disappeared.

A thick liquid now covered their path to

the window. Tom guessed from the smell that it was olive oil.

"To the window! Hurry!" Tom said. "But be careful!"

He sprinted forward and felt his foot slide on the oil. "Whoa!" Tom cried as his legs skated across the floor.

"I've got great balance," Isis boasted. "I'll be fine. You can lean on meeeeee—"

Her left foot slipped and flew out in the opposite direction to her right. Suddenly Isis was doing the splits. Tom tried to pull her up, but slipped again himself. With flailing arms, they skidded round the kitchen on the olive oil.

Just then the two burly guards burst into the kitchen. Catching sight of Tom and Isis, they ran towards the children, not noticing the oil spill. The first guard slipped and fell on his back, the second guard fell and went sliding across the room.

"Aaarrghhh!" the guard screamed. Then with a loud *thump* he hit the kitchen wall.

Tom felt a strong hand grab the back of his tunic, hauling him out of the slippery mush. He looked round and stared straight into the furious face of Prince Paris himself.

"Where do you think you're going, thieves?!" he said. "You stole my father's ring!"

The prince's teeth were set in a grim snarl. Tom was reminded of next door's horrible German shepherd dog.

"Nonsense! What are you talking about?" Isis asked, taking a step towards him.

Tom couldn't help but look directly at the pocket of her tunic, where he was certain she had put the ring. Hopefully Prince Paris wouldn't see it.

"I know you've stolen it, you little dung-hill rat!"

Isis tensed beside Tom. "How DARE you?" she said.

For a second, Paris seemed confused. "Er, I'm the Prince of Troy. So... er... I dare quite easily, actually, SERVANT!"

Isis poked the prince in his tummy. "Go on, then, if you think you're so clever. Search us!"

"Search us?" Tom asked. He stared at Isis, baffled. What on earth was she saying? She was going to get them thrown from the walls of Troy! "No, I *really* don't think Prince Paris needs to search us," he said.

Isis flicked her plaits over her shoulder. "Oh, yes," she said, sticking her nose in the air, "he *really* does!"

She's gone mad, Tom thought.

If Paris found the amulet, they'd never be able to give it to Anubis. Isis would never get to the Afterlife… and Tom would be stuck in ancient Troy forever!

CHAPTER 9
CAT-APULT

Prince Paris shoved Tom's shoulder. "I'll search you first," he said.

"Fine!" Tom said. He held out his arms at the sides as Paris patted him down.

The prince frowned. "Hmm. It seems you're in the clear." He turned to Isis with a nasty grin. "Next!"

Tom watched in horrified silence as the prince yanked Isis's arms roughly in the air.

"You won't find anything," Isis said in a sing-song voice.

"We'll see about that," Paris said. He patted her tunic. "Oh, what have we here? A secret pocket?"

Tom held his breath. His heart galloped. *Will Paris fling us into a pit with wild, hungry*

dogs? How about flogging? Tom was fairly certain a lot of flogging went on in Troy.

But Paris's grin vanished from his face as he finished searching Isis's pockets.

"Nothing? I don't believe it," he said.

He shook his head and stared down at his sandals. "Father must be losing his marbles," he muttered. He looked at Isis in disgust. "Get out of my sight," he said. Then he stormed out of the kitchen.

"Are you OK?" a voice asked.

Tom glanced over to the fire, where Hermon was still tending to Phineus's burn. "Sorry about the mess," Tom said sheepishly, looking down at the oily floor.

"Don't worry about it," Hermon said. "Watching everyone slip and slide was pretty funny."

117

Isis grabbed Tom's hand. "Ready to go?" she asked.

Tom allowed her to drag him towards the back door.

"But the ring..." he whispered. "We can't leave without the ring!"

Isis tapped the side of her nose. "Don't you worry," she said. "Isis Amun-Ra has got everything under control."

Tom crossed his fingers and hoped that she was right.

Waving goodbye to Hermon, they slipped out of the palace through the kitchen door, into the moonlight.

"There she is!" Isis said. She pointed to Cleo, who stood in the middle of a large courtyard. Grand buildings and neat lines of olive trees towered above her on every side. Her meows echoed off the stone. Tom bent over and took a deep breath. "How lucky was that?" he asked. "We got away with it! How did Paris miss the ring in your pocket?"

Isis snorted and started to walk towards Cleo. "*Luck*?! Luck didn't come into it," Isis said, flicking her hair. "He didn't find it, because it wasn't there!"

Cleo padded forward. Her shadow stretched out behind her on the ground. Her tail pointed straight up at the moon.

"Fluffpot!" Isis said gleefully.

"If it wasn't there, where is it—"

But a thunderous noise interrupted Tom's question.

Just then, the Greek army marched smartly into the courtyard. Their armour glinted in the moonlight. Their feet drummed on the flagstones like hard rain.

"Oh no! The battle has finally caught up
with us. Take cover!" Tom told Isis.

He looked round for a good hiding
place and spotted a giant stone fountain
in the middle of the square. In the centre
of the fountain, a bronze sculpture of a

Trojan warrior stood with a sword in one hand and a shield in another. He was tall and forbidding. Water spurted from his mouth.

"Follow me!" Tom said.

"But what about Cleo?" Isis wailed.

"She'll be fine," Tom said.

Sure enough, as Tom and Isis scurried over to hide in the shadows of the fountain, Cleo scrabbled up a nearby olive tree, out of harm's way.

Harsh battle cries rang out through the square. Priam's soldiers streamed out of the palace, waving their swords and spears at the advancing Greeks.

"Charge!" came a familiar, whiny voice above the din.

Tom and Isis peeked over the rim of the fountain.

121

"Odysseus!" Isis whispered.

Arrows whizzed through the air, thudding as they met their targets, or clattering uselessly to the ground.

As the Greeks barrelled into the Trojan soldiers with all their might, Odysseus himself made straight for the fountain. He jumped up on to the wide, marble rim.

"Get down!" Tom hissed to Isis. "He'll see us." Sneaking a peek, he saw Odysseus brandishing his sword at the bronze Trojan that loomed above them in the gloom.

"Take that, you Trojan rat!" Odysseus shouted. He lost his balance and toppled into the water with a *splash*. Then, unaware of the two children that were watching him, he stood tall again. He struck the statue then got squirted right in the eye by the water that spewed

from the statue's mouth. "How dare you spit
at me!" he shouted. "I am Commander of
the Greek army!"

Isis found this so funny that she started to laugh.

Odysseus spun round and pointed his sword straight at both of them.

"You! I recognise you two," he said. "On your feet!"

Tom and Isis stood with their hands raised. Nearby, a Greek warrior and a Trojan warrior battled, their weapons clashing against each other. Dripping wet, Odysseus poked the tip of his sword against Tom's chest.

"You're the Spartan cubs," he said, narrowing his eyes. "You cowardly little deserters! I saw you hiding down there, trying to avoid fighting."

Tom stared open-mouthed at the chief commander. "You're calling *us* cowardly?" he said, trying to sound braver than he actually felt. "And here *you* are, picking a fight with a statue and two children, when you should be fighting big, tough Trojan soldiers?"

Odysseus swung his blade so that it was resting on Tom's shoulder. Tom felt the colour draining from his cheeks as he stared into the Greek hero's face.

"Do you know what I do to deserters?" Odysseus asked.

The glow of the flames that burned in the surrounding buildings made his bronze helmet and armour look as though it was on fire too. The smell of smoke hung thickly in the air, making it hard for Tom to breathe.

He shook his head in silence.

"I chop off their heads!" Odysseus said.

Suddenly Tom heard a furious yowl.
It seemed to come from the night sky.

125

He looked up and saw Cleo leaping down
from the top branch of an olive tree. She
landed with a *thwack* on Odysseus's helmet.
"Aaarrrggghhhh!" wailed Odysseus,
trying to pry off the
cat. "Get this furry
thing away
from me!

ARRRGHHH... CHOOOOOOO!"
Odysseus was knocked backwards by his
giant sneeze and fell with an almighty *splash*
into the fountain.

"Quickly! We've not a moment to lose!"
Isis said, fishing out her cat as Odysseus
splashed about in the water. She held
Cleo tight and said, "Such a brave, brave
Fluffpot."

Tom had to agree with her. Cleo hated
water, and was terrified of heights – but
none of that had mattered when it had
come to saving them.

Isis looked up at Tom. "You were really
brave too," she said.

"Er, thanks," Tom said, surprised.

"But don't go getting a big head," Isis
said, grinning. Then she turned back to
Cleo. "Have you got anything for me?"

Tom gasped as Cleo opened her mouth and dropped the ring into Isis's hand.

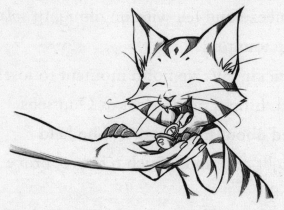

"Clever girl!" Isis cooed. The amulet glowed in the moonlight. "I slipped it to Cleo when we were leaving the throne room," she explained to Tom. "I told you we couldn't leave without her."

Tom, Isis and Cleo joined hands and paws. They all touched the amulet in King Priam's ring. Then a strong wind started to whip round them like a tornado, sucking them out of Troy. The fires that burned in

Priam's palace flickered out of view and Tom felt a strange, tugging feeling, as he left the world of the Ancient Greeks and flew through the twisting tunnels of time.

CHAPTER 10
CHECKING OUT

With a bump, Tom found himself back in
the frozen food aisle of the supermarket. Isis
and Cleo had landed back in the shopping
trolley, wrapped in their mummy bandages
once more.

Isis shivered. "I miss Ancient Greece
already!" she said, rubbing her arms. "But at
least we brought back a nice souvenir!"
she said, waving the yellow amulet at Tom.

Cleo meowed and pawed at the packet of

fish fingers in the trolley.

"Next time Mum makes fish fingers, I'll save you some," Tom promised Cleo, scratching her behind the ears. Without the little cat's help, they'd probably still be stuck in the middle of the Trojan War!

"So good of you to drop in!" Anubis's voice boomed over the supermarket loudspeaker.

Looking round, Tom could see that none of the other shoppers could hear him. And Mum didn't seem to notice that Tom had been on a time-travelling adventure as she was busy ticking things off her shopping list.

"Where are you, you stinky-breathed, dog-faced—?" Isis began to shout up at the speakers that hung from the ceiling. But she was interrupted as the frozen vegetables

started to rumble. Some bags split open,
spurting rock-hard sweetcorn everywhere.
The god of the Underworld burst up out of
the freezer.

"Looking for me?" said Anubis, his jackal face smirking at them.

Isis picked up a bottle of olive oil that was in the trolley and shook it at Anubis. "Nice try with the oil," she said. "But it didn't stop us from getting the amulet."

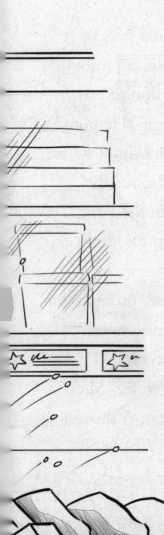

Tom groaned. Why couldn't Isis resist taunting the god?

"I'll take that!" Anubis growled, swiping Priam's ring out of Isis's hand. He slipped it on to his finger and held out his hand in front of him to admire it.

"It looked better on King Priam," grumbled Isis.

"Well, it's MINE now – as it should have been all along," said Anubis. The god glanced round the supermarket. "So much CHOICE," he said, drumming his fingers on the freezer cabinet.

But Tom had a feeling Anubis wasn't deciding what brand of frozen pizza to buy.

"Decisions, decisions. I just don't know where to send you children next." He bared his sharp teeth and snarled. "But don't worry, one thing's for certain – it will make the Trojan War look like a walk in the park!"

Then, before Tom could say anything, Anubis and the ring disappeared.

"Well, that's that," Tom said, pushing the trolley along. "Another adventure over."

"Four down, two to go," Isis replied. "And then *finally* I can get to the Afterlife." She punched the air with excitement. A shower of crusty bandage flakes drifted down into the trolley. *Mum would have a fit if she could see that all the food was covered in ancient mummy dust,* thought Tom.

Mum looked down at the sweetcorn that Anubis had scattered over the floor.

"Did you make this mess?" she asked Tom, putting one hand on her hip.

Tom shook his head, while Isis giggled in the trolley.

"Good. I don't want another argument with the manager!" Mum said.

Tom turned back to Isis and whispered, "I wonder where we *will* end up next."

"How about the sweets aisle?" Isis suggested.

With Mum convinced that nothing out of the ordinary had gone on, Tom pushed Isis towards his favourite section.

"Fruit and nut or milk?" he asked, as they looked at the chocolate.

But Isis wasn't listening. She was sitting in the bottom of the trolley, deep in thought and surrounded by food.

"Poor King Priam," she said, resting her chin in her hand. "I wish we could have saved him."

Tom picked a big bar of milk chocolate off the shelf. "We can give history a nudge in the right direction, but we can't change its course," he said.

"I think he was probably a nice king."

"Why do you say that?" asked Tom, heading towards the checkout, where Mum was standing, waiting in the queue.

"I don't know," said Isis. "But there was something about him that really reminded me of my father."

"But your father was an Egyptian pharaoh. Wasn't he a lot younger than King Priam, too?"

"YEEEEESSSS," Isis said, sounding annoyed. "I said he reminded me of my father. Not that he looked like him or anything. *Obviously!*"

Tom wanted to say something cutting back, but he knew Isis hadn't seen her own family for over five thousand years. Nor would she, until she got to the Afterlife.

In a quiet voice, Isis explained. "I just meant that he seemed nice – like my father."

Tom thought about how much he'd miss his own dad if he couldn't see him. And his mum too. He desperately wanted to cheer Isis up. "Don't worry, you'll be in the Afterlife soon – we'll find those last two amulets, I promise."

He held up the bar of chocolate. "And in the meantime, try some of this!"

Isis and Tom both munched big squares of chocolate.

"Yum!" said Isis, chocolate dribbling on to her bandages, "I hope there are sweets in the Afterlife…"

As Mum chatted to the lady on the checkout, Tom packed the shopping into bags and Isis polished off the rest of the bar.

The chocolate certainly seemed to be doing the trick. Isis stood up in the trolley and laughed mischievously.

Tom looked nervously at her. "What are you up to, Isis?" he asked.

Cleo scrambled into the child seat and meowed with excitement.

"Giddy up, horsey!" Isis shouted.

Tom grinned and set off at a jog, pushing Princess Isis and Cleo on a chariot ride to the supermarket car park.

Tom didn't know where Anubis would send them on their next time-travelling adventure, but one thing was for sure – with Isis and Cleo around, even a trip to the supermarket became an adventure!

TURN THE PAGE TO . . .

- ➤ Meet the REAL Greek warriors!
- ➤ Find out fantastic FACTS!
- ➤ Battle with your GAMING CARDS!
- ➤ And MUCH MORE!

WHO WERE THE MIGHTIEST GREEK WARRIORS?

Odysseus was actually a *real* soldier Find out more about him and other brave Greek warriors.

ODYSSEUS was the king of Ithaca, a Greek island. He is the hero of two epic poems about the Trojan War. In *The Illiad*, Odysseus's cleverness helps the Greek army win the ten-year war against Troy. It was Odysseus's idea to build a giant wooden horse for the Greek soldiers to hide in so they could sneak inside the city walls. Neat trick!

GREEKS
ODYSSEUS

Brain Power	400
Fear Factor	280
Bravery	380
Weapon: Bow and Arrow	260

— TOTAL 1320 —

HECTOR was King Priam's oldest son. He was the Trojan army's greatest warrior — even the Greeks admired him for his courage, skill and honour. He disagreed with the war between the Greeks and Trojans, but he still bravely defended the city of Troy. He challenged the Greek warriors to a one-on-one fight and Ajax, a Greek hero, was chosen as his opponent. The fight went on for a whole day and ended in a draw. Ajax was so impressed with Hector that he gave him his own sash. Hector gave Ajax his sword in return. What great sports!

GREEKS
HECTOR

Brain Power	295
Fear Factor	320
Bravery	340
Weapon: Sword	300

— TOTAL 1255 —

ACHILLES was the Greek army's best warrior. He was said to be born invincible (except for a spot on his heel) – so he had quite an advantage over mere mortals! Achilles defeated many of the

GREEKS
ACHILLES

Brain Power	275
Fear Factor	340
Bravery	250
Weapon: Spear	190
TOTAL	1055

Trojans' best fighters. It was Achilles who defeated Hector, after the Trojan prince killed his best friend. Achilles was in turn killed when Hector's brother, Paris, shot an arrow into his heel. Today we use the expression Achilles' heel to mean someone's weak spot.

AJAX was the great-grandson of the Greek god Zeus. Ajax was said to be as tall as a tower and the strongest of all the Greek warriors. His combat skills were second only to his cousin Achilles's and he was never wounded in battle. When Achilles died, Ajax wanted his magical armour but Odysseus got it instead. Ajax was so upset that he fell on his own sword and died. A bit of an overreaction!

Brain Power	290
Fear Factor	255
Bravery	210
Weapon: Javelin	180

— TOTAL **935** —

WEAPONS

The epic story of the Siege of Troy features many battles and one-on-one fights between heroic soldiers. Both armies used many different weapons when attacking or defending.

Spear: a long wooden pole with a sharp metal point in the shape of a leaf. It was the main weapon of choice for Greek soldiers.

Xiphos sword: a double-edged sword that was shaped like a leaf.

Shield: two types of shield were used by Greek soldiers – the hoplon shield was made from heavy wood, and the pelte shield was made from wicker so it was lighter to carry (this shield was used by soldiers who needed to attack with speed and surprise).

Phalanx: an army formation used when defending. Soldiers would stand tightly together armed with shields and spears.

GREEK WARRIORS TIMELINE

In GREEK WARRIORS Tom and Isis go to Ancient Greece, which was made up of lots of different states, who often fought against each other, as well as other countries. Discover more in this brilliant timeline!

490 BC
Persia invades Athens but is beaten by the Greek army at the Battle of Marathon.

1250 BC
The Trojan War.

776 BC
The first Olympic games are held in Olympia.

460–445 BC
First war between Athens and Sparta.

Ding ding!
Round two.

336 BC

Alexander the Great becomes the king of Macedon, in northern Greece. He creates an empire from Greece to the Himalayas.

431–404 BC

Second war – more fighting between Athens and Sparta!

323 BC

Alexander the Great dies and his empire is divided.

430 BC

The Great Plague of Athens kills a quarter of the entire population.

330 BC

The first 'camera obscura' is invented by Aristotle. It was a type of pinhole camera that all modern cameras are based on.

TIME HUNTERS TIMELINE

Tom and Isis never know where in history they'll go to next!
Check out in what order their adventures *actually* happen.

3100 – 1070 BC
Ancient Egypt

300 BC – AD 476
Ancient Rome

776 – 323 BC
Ancient Greece

AD 1000 – 1300
Medieval England

AD 789 – 1066
The Age of the
Vikings

AD 1500 – 1830
Era of piracy in
the Caribbean

FANTASTIC FACTS

Impress your friends with these facts about
Ancient Greece.

➤ The Battle of Marathon was a famous
Greek victory against the Persians. A
Greek hero called Pheidippides ran 150
miles to fetch help from Sparta. After
the battle he ran 26 miles to Athens
to tell them the good news, but then
he died of exhaustion. This is why the
modern marathon race is 26 miles long.
Even reading this makes me tired!

➤ The yo-yo was
invented in
Ancient Greece
and is one of the
oldest toys in the world. *Cool!*

➜ Some Greeks would not eat beans
because they thought they had the
souls of the dead in them.
What a great excuse!

➜ Spartans were the fiercest
and toughest of the Greek
warriors. They had a
special drink made from
salt, vinegar and blood.
How disgusting!

➜ The Olympics were invented in
Ancient Greece in a city called
Olympia. Athletes
would compete
naked.
Well that would be
embarrassing in P.E....

WHO IS THE MIGHTIEST?

Collect the Gaming Cards and play!

Battle with a friend to find out which historical hero is the mightiest of them all!

Players: 2
Number of Cards: 4+ each

➤ Players start with an equal number of cards. Decide which player goes first.

➤ Player 1: choose a category from your first card (Brain Power, Fear Factor, Bravery or Weapon), and read out the score.

➤ Player 2: read out the stat from the same category on your first card.

➤ The player with the highest score wins the round, takes their opponent's card and puts it at the back of their own pack.

➤ The winning player then chooses a category from the next card and play continues.

➤ The game continues until one player has won all the cards. The last card played wins the title 'Mightiest hero of them all!'

GREEKS

HECTOR

Brain Power	
Fear Factor	295
Bravery	320
Weapon: Sword	340
	300

— TOTAL 1255 —

For more fantastic games go to:
www.time-hunters.com

BATTLE THE MIGHTIEST!

Collect a new set of mighty warriors — free in every Time Hunters book! Have you got them all?

GLADIATORS

- [ ] Hilarus
- [ ] Spartacus
- [ ] Flamma
- [ ] Emperor Commodus

KNIGHTS

- [ ] King Arthur
- [ ] Galahad
- [ ] Lancelot
- [ ] Gawain

VIKINGS

- [ ] Erik the Red
- [ ] Harald Bluetooth
- [ ] Ivar the Boneless
- [ ] Canute the Great

GREEKS

- [ ] Hector
- [ ] Ajax
- [ ] Achilles
- [ ] Odysseus

Coming soon!

PIRATES

- [ ] Blackbeard
- [ ] Captain Kidd
- [ ] Henry Morgan
- [ ] Calico Jack

EGYPTIANS

- [ ] Anubis
- [ ] King Tut
- [ ] Isis
- [ ] Tom

Who was Captain Blackbeard?
Did people really have to walk the plank?
And where was Davy Jones' locker?

Join Tom and Isis on another action-packed
Time Hunters adventure!

They had landed on a perfect sandy beach
in a deserted bay. Palm trees heavy with
coconuts nodded in a light sea breeze. The
blue sea lapped gently against the sand.

She's right, Tom thought, chuckling to

himself. *This place isn't bad. Maybe Anubis has sent us on a tropical holiday.*

Tom looked down at his linen shirt and baggy breeches. "Look! My trunks have gone!" he said.

Isis tugged at her clothes. "What are these ridiculous outfits, exactly?" she asked.

Tom felt the frill on his shirt. "Not sure," he said, frowning. "I don't like the girly ruffles, though."

Isis lay back on the warm sand with her arms behind her head. She looked at Tom with sparkling brown eyes that were lined with kohl. "This sunshine is just like being back home in Egypt," she said, sighing happily. "So much nicer than cold and rainy old Britain. Never mind the Afterlife. Let's just stay here! We can relax all day long and eat fresh fish and drink coconut milk!"

Cleo mewed in agreement before running off to chase crabs.

Tom leaped up. "Not a chance," he said. "Come on! Let's go exploring!"

After an hour of wandering in the hot sun, Isis didn't seem to be enjoying the heat any more.

"I'm thirsty," she moaned, grabbing her throat. "You have to find me some water."

But as the three of them rounded the cove, Isis suddenly fell silent. Tom stared at the row of shop fronts and inns that lined the next bay along. They were all painted in pretty pastel colours. In the distance, people hurried along the promenade.

"I wonder what kind of place this is?" Isis said.

Tom gazed out to where large ships were

anchored in the deeper water. Suddenly he spotted their flags, showing skulls, crossbones and cutlasses. He gulped.

"Pirates!" Tom said under his breath.

Isis's eyes widened. "Pirates?" she asked, raising an eyebrow. "We had those back in my day."

"I'm pretty sure we're not in Ancient Egypt," said Tom. He sheltered his eyes from the glare of the sun with his hand. "Those ships look like French or Dutch galleons," he said. "I've seen them in books and films."

Tom was about to ask Isis if she had ever seen the film *Pirates of the Caribbean*, but he realised how silly that would sound to someone who had lived five thousand years ago.

"So where are we then?" Isis asked, as she scratched Cleo behind the ears.

"I think we're in the eighteenth century," Tom said. "Pirates were a massive problem in those days. They were always attacking ships carrying things like gold."

"Gold?" Isis asked, wide-eyed.

"You bet!" Tom said. "The Caribbean Sea was where all the big pirate battles happened."

"How could anyone want to fight when they're living here?" Isis said, looking at the beautiful view.

"Look, forget the scenery!" Tom said. "We really need to ask your scarab ring for some help if we're ever going to find the fifth amulet."

Isis nodded and stroked the magical golden scarab that sat on her finger. On it was a picture of the goddess Isis, whom Isis was named after. The ring had given Tom and

Isis clues about where the first four amulets had been hidden. "Goddess Isis," Isis began. "Please, please help us once more! Tell us where we can find the fifth amulet."

Silvery words flew up out of the ring and hung in the air in a riddle.

Tom read it out to Isis:

"To seek this jewel, shining greeny-blue,
In a Spaniard's chest of bullion,
First you must join the ragged crew,
As the Teacher's lowly scullion.
His whiskers threaten like a thundercloud,
He's the high seas' worst rapscallion,
But he'll help you pinch it from the crab,
Within sight of the red cross galleon."

Isis sighed. "I haven't got a clue what any of that means," she said. "I never do.

Explain, Professor Smartypants!"

"Well, it mentions a Spaniard," Tom said. "Most of the Caribbean islands were ruled by the Spanish. Not sure about the rest, but it sounds like we've got to look for a man with a hairy, scary face! Maybe the red cross means we'll find him at a hospital."

Tom, Isis and Cleo set off walking towards the busy harbour.

"What's a 'rapscallion'?" Isis asked.

"My grandad uses that word," Tom said. "I think it means that we're after a bad guy."

Before they'd gone far, they crossed paths with a young man. He was running so fast that he almost crashed right into them.

"Watch it!" Tom said.

The young man adjusted the red scarf that was tied around his long dark hair. He wore the same kind of breeches and shirt as Tom and Isis, except that his were covered in stains.

"Sorry!" he said, frowning. "What's a pair of nippers doing in a dangerous hole like New Providence?"

"Is that where we are?" Tom asked. He had heard about New Providence in his history books. It was a famous pirate port.

The young man nodded. "Of course! You two need to get yourselves home sharpish, before you run into trouble."

"Oh, we can't," Tom said, thinking fast. "We've been, er… shipwrecked. Our parents were lost at sea, but we clung to some wood and floated to this island."

Isis pulled a sad face and sniffed, adding, "We don't have a home to go back to…"

The young man held out his hand. "Salmagundi's the name. Sal for short. I'm sorry to hear about your troubles."

Tom shook Sal's hand. "I'm Tom, this is Isis, and her cat, Cleo."

"Listen," Sal said, leaning in. His tanned face made his green eyes look slightly wild. "Not everyone here on New Providence is nice. So stick by me, OK? I'll take you to the Jolly Barnacle Inn. I do the cooking there. But one day I'm going to be a pirate."

Tom and Isis exchanged excited glances.

He straightened up and peered at the sun. "But we'd better hurry, because if I don't get a move on, I'll be getting fifty of the owner's best."

"Best what?" Isis asked.

"Fifty lashes. With a whip!"

"Ouch!" said Isis, wincing.

As Tom, Isis and Cleo followed Sal into the port, Tom saw that the row of shops wasn't very pretty close-up. There was broken glass in the window frames and rotten vegetables all over the ground.

"Yuck!" he said to Isis. "What a pong."

Isis nodded, holding her shirt over her nose.

They arrived at the Jolly Barnacle Inn,
with its sign hung crookedly over the door.
As soon as they stepped inside, a finely
dressed pirate with the most rotten teeth Tom
had ever seen hurled a bar stool at another
mean-looking, muscly man.

"Are you sayin' I look like a girl?" the
elegant pirate said. He cocked his pistol and
fired it at the ceiling, so that plaster showered
down.

The muscly pirate laughed heartily. "You
look so much like a woman, they won't let
you back on your own ship with the real
men!" He smacked the pistol out of the first
pirate's hand.

"I'll slit your gizzard for that!" the first

pirate cried, drawing his cutlass.

Crumbs, Tom thought. *Talk about overreacting*.

Tom, Isis, Cleo and Sal edged past the fighting pair.

"Never insult a pirate if you value your life," Sal advised them.

He led them to an empty table in the corner. "Sit here, and try to stay out of everyone's way," he said. "I'll find you a little something to eat."

As Sal disappeared into the kitchen, Isis looked round and wrinkled her nose.

"This place is disgusting," she said loudly. She poked the tabletop and shuddered. "Yuck. It's sticky."

"Then don't touch it!" Tom said.

"This place isn't fit for a princess!" Isis protested.

Tom lowered his voice to whisper. "Keep your voice down. I'm not sure these pirates would take kindly to you insulting their favourite hang-out."

Sal returned and slammed two tankards down on the table. "Grog," he announced. "Drink up!"

Tom sipped the drink... and immediately spat it out.

"Ugh! Sal, what do they put in this? Washing-up liquid?" he cried.

"No idea what you're talking about, shipmate. It'll put hairs on your chest."

Sal swigged the contents of his tankard. Grog poured down the sides of his chin and on to his shirt. Then he went back to work in the kitchen.

Pretending to drink, Tom and Isis listened to what was being said by a scary-looking group of pirates at the next table.

"So, Jones tells me there be a Spanish merchant ship leaving Cuba," one man said, glancing round to make sure no one else was listening.

"What's it carrying?" another asked, scratching his nose with his dagger hilt. "Will there be rum and spices and sugar and—"

"Aye," the first man said, nodding. "And cotton too. But listen..." he looked round again, then whispered, "It's got a chest full of gold!"

"Ooooooh!" the other pirates gasped.

Tom was just about to nudge Isis when there was a crash, followed by gunshots. Tom turned round and saw a huge, fearsome man standing in the doorway pointing a gun into the room. He had the biggest, blackest beard Tom had ever seen. His bushy whiskers were plaited with colourful ribbons at the end. Tom gulped.

Suddenly every man in the inn started screaming as loud bangs, pops and flashes of light exploded round the man.

"We're under attack!" Sal yelled.

Tom dived to the floor, and pulled Isis down with him. A terrified Cleo leaped into Isis's arms.

"Under the table – quick!" Tom said.

As he, Isis and Cleo hid beneath the table, another explosion went off with a terrifying BANG!

THE HUNT CONTINUES...

Travel through time with Tom and Isis as they battle the mightiest warriors of the past. Will they find all six amulets, or will Isis be banished from the Afterlife forever?
Find out in:

Got it! ☐

Got it! ☐

Got it! ☐

Got it!

☐

Got it!

☐

Got it!

☐

Tick off the books as you collect them!

Go to:

www.time-hunters.com

Travel through time and join the hunt for the mightiest heroes and villains of history to win **brilliant prizes!**

For more adventures, awesome card games, competitions and thrilling news, scan this QR code*:

*If you have a smartphone you can download a free QR code reader from your app store